AN ILLUSTRATED COLLECTION OF

FAIRY TALES

FOR BRAVE CHILDREN

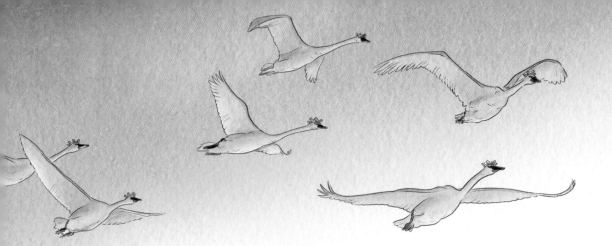

An Illustrated Collection of
Fairy Tales
for Brave Children

ILLUSTRATED BY
SCOTT PLUMBE

Floris
Books

For Rosemary, Sam and Cole,
who bring storytime to life every night – S.P.

The illustrations in this book are sketched in pencil
and combined with ink and watercolour digitally

Originally published in German as *Grimmig und anders:
Gruselmärchen aus aller Welt* by Esslinger Verlag, Stuttgart
First published in English by Floris Books in 2020
© 2017 Esslinger part of Thienemann-Esslinger Verlag GmbH
English text © 2020 Floris Books
www.florisbooks.co.uk
British Library CIP Data available. ISBN 978-178250-671-3
Printed in Malaysia by Tien Wah Press

Floris Books supports sustainable forest management
by printing this book on materials made from wood that
comes from responsible sources and reclaimed material

CONTENTS

THE SPIRIT
IN THE BOTTLE

There was once a poor woodcutter who worked from early morning till late at night. When he had finally saved a little money, he said to his son, "I've earned a bit extra from working hard, and as you're my only child, I'm going to spend it on your education. Then, if you learn a decent trade, you'll be able to look after me in my old age."

The boy went away to school and studied hard. But before he had completed his learning, his father's savings ran out and he had to return home.

One morning, as his father was preparing to go to work, the boy said, "Why don't I come along and help you?"

The woodcutter was unsure. "You're not used to heavy work, and anyway, I only have one axe."

But the boy suggested they borrow an axe from their neighbour, which they did, before going to the forest together. The boy chopped wood happily, until the sun was high in the sky and his father said, "Let's rest and have something to eat."

"You rest, Father," said the boy. "I'm going to look for birds' nests."

He walked deep into the forest, until he came to a huge old oak tree. 'A tree this size must be full of nests,' he thought.

Suddenly he heard a muffled cry: "Let me out, let me out!"

"Who's there?" he asked.

"Look among the tree roots!" called the voice.

The boy searched and found a glass bottle. He held it up to the light, and saw something moving inside. "Let me out. Let me out!" it wailed.

Seeing no reason not to, the boy pulled the cork out of the bottle. In a flash, a spirit slipped out, and grew as big as the oak tree. "Your reward for freeing me," he thundered, "is a broken neck!"

"You should have told me that before," the boy said fearlessly. "I'd like to keep my neck as it is."

"I'm sure you would, but I am the mighty Mercurius, and when somebody sets me free, I must break their neck."

"Wait!" the boy cried. He thought fast. "You're huge. Prove you were really in the bottle, then you can give me my reward."

"Fine," the spirit replied haughtily, shrinking himself down.

No sooner was he inside the bottle again than the boy replaced the cork and tossed it among the roots of the tree.

The spirit had been outsmarted.

"You are indeed a clever young man," said the spirit from inside the bottle. "Free me again and I won't hurt you. I promise you a true reward that will last a lifetime."

'Perhaps he will keep his word?' thought the boy. Mustering his courage and hoping for good luck, he pulled the cork.

Out came the spirit, who again grew large, and then handed the boy a piece of cloth. "This is your reward. Rub a wound with one end, and it will be healed; rub iron or steel with the other end, and it will turn to silver."

The boy tried cutting the bark of a tree, then rubbing it with the cloth. The bark regrew. Happy with his gift, he thanked the spirit and went back to his father.

"Where have you been all this time?" asked the woodcutter angrily when the boy returned. "What about your work?"

"Don't worry, Father. Just watch, I'll fell this tree in no time," said the boy, lifting the axe and striking a powerful blow. But the hard iron blade had rubbed against his magic cloth and turned to soft silver, so the axe bent.

The boy was shocked and his father was horrified. "Now I'll have to find money to pay for the broken axe!" the woodcutter groaned.

"Don't be angry," replied the boy, "I'll pay for it."

"You fool! You might think you're smart, but you know nothing of money, or cutting down trees," replied the woodcutter.

Next day, the woodcutter's anger had faded. "Go and see if you can get a few pennies for that ruined axe in town," he said.

The boy took the silver axe to the goldsmith, who weighed it and gave him four hundred coins.

When he got home, his pockets heavy, the boy told his father to give their neighbour double whatever he asked for the loss of his axe. "Father, we're so rich you'll never have to chop wood again. Look!"

"Good lord," exclaimed the woodcutter, "where did you get all that money?"

The boy told his father about outsmarting the spirit, and his magical reward. He used the rest of the money to return to school. And he healed so many wounds with his cloth that he became a famous doctor, known far and wide.

THE SELFISH GIANT

Once there was an enormous giant's castle beside a small village. The giant had been away for many years.

Every day after school, the village children played in the castle garden. It was a large and lovely garden, with soft green grass, beautiful flowers and peach trees that bore delicate blossoms in spring and rich fruit in autumn.

But then the giant came back.

15

He had been to visit his friend the Cornish ogre. Striding up to his castle, the giant found children playing all around it.

"What are you doing here?" he shouted, and the frightened children ran away.

"My own garden is my own garden," said the giant, "and I will allow nobody to play in it but me." So he built a high wall around it and put up a sign that read:

TRESPASSERS WILL BE EATEN

He was a very selfish giant.

The poor children had nowhere to play. They would wander around the high wall when their lessons were over, and remember the beautiful garden inside.

"I loved the flowers and trees," they said to each other.

Then spring came, and everywhere was alive with blossoms and birds. Yet in the garden of the selfish giant it was still winter. Because there were no children, the birds did not sing and the trees did not bloom.

The snow and the frost were the only ones who were pleased. "Spring has forgotten this garden," they cried, "so we will live here all year round." The snow covered the grass with her great white cloak, and the frost painted all the trees silver.

Then they invited the north wind. Wrapped in furs, he roared around the garden all day. "This is a delightful spot," he said. "We must ask the hail to visit." So the hail came too. Dressed in grey, her breath was like ice. She rattled on the roof of the castle until she broke most of the slates, then stormed about the garden in a flurry.

"I cannot understand why spring is so late in coming," said the selfish giant, as he looked out at his cold white garden. "I hope there will be a change in the weather."

But spring never came, nor summer. The autumn gave fruit to every orchard, but to the giant's garden she gave none. "He is too selfish," she said. So it was always winter there, and the north wind and the hail and the frost and the snow danced through the bare trees.

One morning the giant woke to the sound of a bird singing outside his window. Surprised, he peered out and saw that the hail had stopped dancing and the north wind had ceased roaring. "Spring has come at last!" he cried.

Through a little hole in the wall, the children had crept into the garden. They were sitting in the branches of the trees, which were covered with blossom. Birds twittered with delight, and the flowers danced.

But in one corner, it was still winter. A little boy stood crying by a snow-covered tree. He was so small he couldn't reach the branches.

The giant's heart melted. "How selfish I have been! I will knock down the wall, and my garden shall be the children's playground forevermore."

But when the children saw the giant, they ran away and winter returned. Only the little boy remained. The giant gently lifted him into the tree, and it burst into bloom. Unafraid, the boy flung his arms around the giant's neck and kissed him.

When the other children saw, they came running back, and spring came with them. "It is your garden now, children," said the giant, and he knocked down the wall.

The children played all day.

When they said goodbye, the giant asked for the small boy who hadn't been afraid.

"He's gone," the children answered.

And though they returned to play every afternoon, they never saw the little boy again.

Years later, when the giant had grown very old, he looked out one winter morning at a wondrous sight.

In the farthest corner of the snowy garden was a tree covered with white blossoms, despite the cold. Underneath stood the little boy from long ago.

The giant rushed to him, asking, "Are you alright? You are still a boy… Who are you?"

"I am the child of love," he answered.

The giant was filled with wonder and knelt before the boy, who smiled and said, "You let me play in your garden once. Today you shall come with me to mine, in Paradise."

When the village children came to play that afternoon, the giant had gone. They found his body under the tree, covered with white blossoms.

THE THREE
GOLDEN HAIRS

There was once a poor couple who had a son. A visiting fortune teller foretold that the baby would always be lucky and would marry the king's daughter.

The king heard about this, and it made him angry. He was a wicked king, but pretended to be kind. "Give me your child," he said to the couple. "I shall take care of him." At first they refused, but when he offered a great deal of gold they agreed, believing the boy's luck would keep him safe.

The king put the child in a box and threw the box in the river. But instead of sinking, it drifted till it reached a mill dam downriver. The miller pulled it out and found the beautiful baby boy inside. He and his wife had no children of their own. They took the child in, bringing him up to be good and true.

Years later, the king was caught in a storm and took shelter in the mill. He asked the miller if the grown boy was his son. "No," the miller replied. "He's a foundling. He floated downriver to us in a box."

The king realised with dismay that it was the lucky boy. He asked the boy to carry a letter to the queen, and wrote a message to his wife that said: *As soon as the boy bearing this letter arrives, kill him.*

The boy set off, but lost his way. At nightfall, he knocked on the door of a forest hut. There was an old woman inside, alone by the fire.

"I'm delivering a letter to the queen," he said, "but I got lost. Could I spend the night here?"

"You poor boy," she said. "This is a thieves' den. If they return, they may kill you."

"I'm not afraid, and I'm too tired to go on," said the boy, and he lay down and fell asleep.

A little later, the thieves returned. "Who's that?" they asked angrily.

"Just a lost boy," the old woman replied. "He's taking a letter to the queen."

The thieves opened the king's message, and when they saw that the boy was to be killed, they felt sorry for him. So they tore it up and wrote another, which said the boy carrying the letter should marry the princess straightaway. Next morning, they showed him the way to the palace.

The queen received the message and followed the instructions, arranging a magnificent wedding. And since the boy was good and true, the princess married him happily.

But after a while, the king came home and saw that the fortune teller's prophecy had been fulfilled. "How could this happen?" he asked, and the queen showed him the letter she'd received.

The furious king decided to get rid of the boy for good. He set a task he thought was impossible and deadly: "If you love my daughter," he commanded, "you must journey to the underworld and bring me three golden hairs from Hades' head."

"I'm not afraid," the boy replied, and he set out on his quest.

The boy came to a city. The watchman stopped him and asked what
he knew.

"Everything," the boy replied.

"In that case, why has the fountain in our marketplace gone dry?"
asked the watchman. "It used to flow with wine."

"I will tell you on my return," replied the boy.

He came to another city, and again the watchman asked him what
he knew.

"Everything," he replied.

"Then why won't this tree flourish? It used to bear golden apples."

"I will tell you on my return," replied the boy.

He travelled on and came to a river. The ferryman asked him what he knew.

"Everything," the boy replied.

"Why must I cross back and forth without anyone to relieve me?" asked the ferryman.

"I will tell you on my return," replied the boy.

After crossing the river, he entered the underworld and found Hades' grandmother. She didn't look very fierce.

"Hades is away," she said. "What is it you want?"

"I need three golden hairs from Hades' head to prove my love."

"That's a lot to ask," she said. "But I like your courage, so I'll help."

"Thank you," he said, "but there are also three things I'd like to know: why a fountain that used to flow with wine has dried up; why a tree that used to bear golden apples won't flourish; and why a ferryman must cross back and forth without relief."

"Those are difficult questions," she said, "but listen carefully, and you'll have your answers." She clicked her fingers and turned him into an ant. "Hide in the folds of my skirt and you'll be safe."

When Hades returned, he took a nap. Carefully, the old woman plucked a golden hair. He woke and cried, "What are you doing?"

"I was dreaming and grabbed your hair," she lied. "I dreamed that a fountain which used to flow with wine had dried up. Why do you think that is?"

"There's a toad sitting in the fountain," he replied. "Kill it and the wine will flow."

She waited until he fell asleep again, then pulled out the second hair.

"Ow! What this time?"

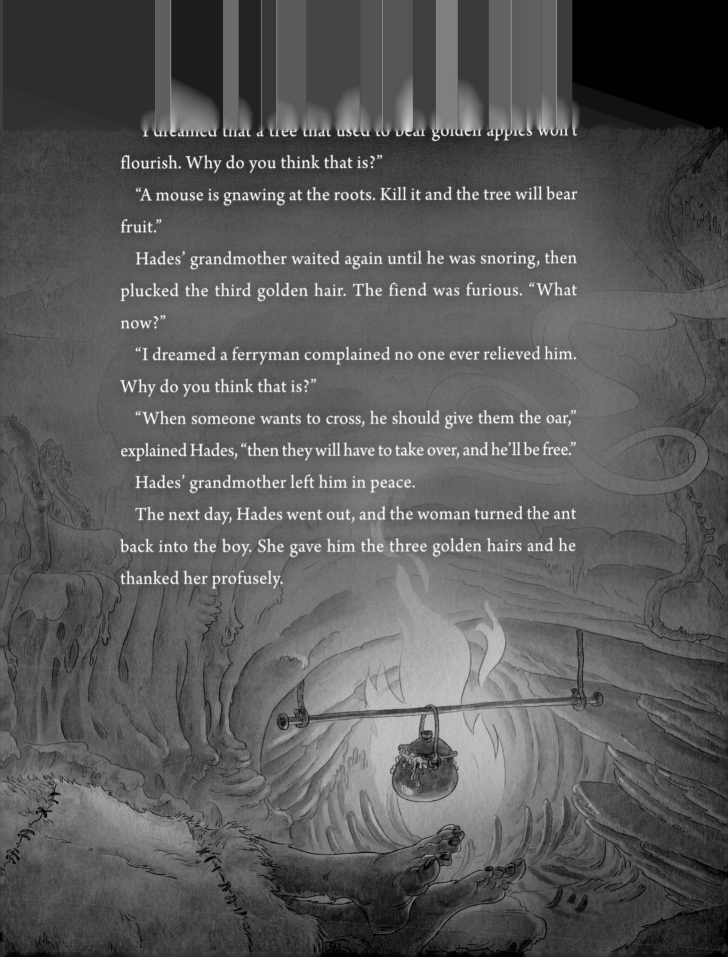

I dreamed that a tree that used to bear golden apples won't flourish. Why do you think that is?"

"A mouse is gnawing at the roots. Kill it and the tree will bear fruit."

Hades' grandmother waited again until he was snoring, then plucked the third golden hair. The fiend was furious. "What now?"

"I dreamed a ferryman complained no one ever relieved him. Why do you think that is?"

"When someone wants to cross, he should give them the oar," explained Hades, "then they will have to take over, and he'll be free."

Hades' grandmother left him in peace.

The next day, Hades went out, and the woman turned the ant back into the boy. She gave him the three golden hairs and he thanked her profusely.

The boy left the underworld and crossed the river with the ferryman. "Give the oar to the next passenger," he said, "then you'll be free."

He came to the city with the barren apple tree and told the watchman about the mouse. To thank him, the watchman gave him two donkeys carrying sacks of gold.

Then the boy came to the city with the dry fountain and told the watchman there about the toad. This watchman also thanked him with two gold-laden donkeys.

At last the boy returned to his princess, who was overjoyed to see him. He gave the outraged king the three hairs, but when the king saw the gold, his anger turned to greed. "Where did you find this?" he asked.

"It comes from a golden riverbank," said the boy. "A ferryman will take you across to it."

The greedy king hurried to the river. The ferryman took him across, then handed the king the oar.

From then on, the king ferried people across the river as punishment for his cruelty and greed, while the lucky boy and his princess lived happily ever after.

THE WILD SWANS

There was once a king who had eleven sons and one daughter, Elisa. Their mother had died when they were very young, yet they grew up happy because they had each other.

But then the king married a wicked queen, who hated the children and plotted to be rid of them. She sent Elisa away to the country to live with farmers until she grew up, then put a terrible curse on the princes: "You shall become great voiceless birds and fly away into the world!" And so the eleven princes were transformed into eleven wild swans.

The swans flew from the palace and circled the countryside until they found the farm where Elisa was living. They hovered over the roof, beating their wings, but by the time their sister came outside, they had gone. Elisa stood alone, playing with a leaf. Holding it up, she thought she could see her brothers' bright eyes.

A few years later, Elisa turned fifteen, and she returned home. When the wicked queen saw how lovely her stepdaughter had become, she was determined to have her banished for ever.

Early one morning the queen snuck into Elisa's bathroom. She took three toads and kissed each one, weaving a dark spell: "Sit upon Elisa and make her so changed that her father will not know her." When Elisa went for her bath, the first toad climbed onto her hair, the second onto her forehead, and the third her shoulder. But because Elisa was so good, the queen's witchcraft had no power, and the toads turned into beautiful red poppies.

The queen was furious. She ripped Elisa's clothes, tangled her auburn hair and rubbed a foul ointment on her face.

The king didn't recognise Elisa when he saw her. Horrified at the girl's appearance, he declared that she could not be his dear daughter. No one in the palace realised who she was.

With sadness in her heart, Elisa slipped away from the castle. She wandered over fields and hills, weeping as she thought of the eleven brothers with whom she had always felt at home. She vowed to find them, however long it might take.

At nightfall she came to a great forest. She lay down on a bed of moss, with glow-worms twinkling around her like stars. All night long Elisa dreamed of her brothers and their happy, carefree childhood together.

The sun was already high when she woke, so she washed in a woodland pool and set out again, without knowing where she should go.

She had walked only a few steps when an old woman appeared, carrying a basket of berries. "Good morning, have you seen eleven princes riding through the forest?" asked Elisa.

"No," replied the old woman, "but earlier I saw eleven swans with golden crowns swimming down a stream close by."

Elisa wondered about the swans and thought she would follow the stream. Eventually she came out upon an open shore. With the unending sea stretching before her, she could go no further.

Weary, she began to weep. Then, through her tears she saw eleven swans' feathers lying on the sand. She gathered them together and decided to sit and wait until the swans returned. Perhaps she could ask them about her brothers.

As the sun dipped low, eleven swans with golden crowns flew towards the shore. Elisa climbed up a nearby dune and hid while they landed, flapping their great wings. Then, when the sun set, the swans' feathery wings transformed and there stood her eleven brothers!

She ran into their arms, calling each by name. The princes were overjoyed to see their little sister, who had become so tall and lovely. They laughed and cried and held each other tight. The eldest brother told Elisa of their curse.

"While the sun is in the sky we must live as wild swans, but at night we return to our human form. We must always find somewhere to rest at sunset, for as men we would fall from the clouds. Tomorrow we fly to a new home across the sea. Do you have the courage to come with us, sister?"

"Oh, yes!" Elisa cried.

And so all night they worked to make a basket from willow twigs and rushes to carry Elisa. When they were finished, she lay down upon it and fell sound asleep.

At sunrise the princes turned back into swans. They gripped the basket in their beaks and carried their sleeping sister over the sea.

When Elisa woke, they were far from land. She thought she was
dreaming, for they soared so high that the ships below looked as
small as seagulls.

Elisa's brothers were headed for a small rock in the middle of the sea where they would stop to rest. But towards the day's end, a storm rolled in. With the buffeting winds and the extra weight of carrying Elisa, they could not fly fast enough. In darkness they would become men, and Elisa thought they would all surely drown in the waves.

When the daylight was nearly gone, the little rock came into view. Elisa willed her brothers to fly faster, harder! Plunging downward, they finally touched solid ground just as night fell.

The rock was very small, and the storm battered them from all sides, but Elisa and her brothers huddled together to give each other courage.

The next day was clear and bright, and the swans flew on, carrying Elisa in her basket. Just before evening, she looked down and saw land. Far below there were towns and castles, and beautiful blue mountains with forests of cedar. The swans landed in a wood at sunset, and set Elisa down by a cave hung with delicate green plants where they could all sleep.

"I wonder what you'll dream of tonight, sister," said the youngest prince.

"If only I could dream of how to free you," Elisa replied.

When Elisa finally slept, an enchanted fairy came to her. She looked strangely like the old woman with the berries who had told Elisa about the wild swans.

"Your brothers can be freed," the fairy said, "but you must be brave. See the stinging nettle in my hand? Gather only this kind and those that grow in graveyards. Though they will blister your skin, you must crush them, spin the flax and knit it into eleven tunics. If these are worn by the wild swans, the spell will be broken. But you must do all this in silence. If you speak, your words will pierce your brothers' hearts like a sword."

When Elisa woke, there on the floor was a pile of nettles like those from her dream. Immediately she began her task. The nettles gave her blisters, yet she knew she could endure any pain to free her brothers.

The princes were distressed by Elisa's silence and the sight of her hands, but they understood that her work was for them. The youngest brother wept, and where his tears fell, Elisa's blisters disappeared.

The next day, as Elisa sat knitting the first tunic, the sound of hunting horns rang through the forest. A party of huntsmen appeared, and the handsome young king of the country was among them.

"Why are you hiding here?" he asked Elisa.

But Elisa dared not speak to him, for she could not risk the lives of her brothers.

"Come with me to safety," said the kind king. He was instantly captivated by Elisa, and concerned about her, and he took her on his horse to his magnificent palace.

Elisa was dressed in fine silks and given special delicacies to eat, yet her only thought was for her brothers. She was desperate to return to her nettle spinning, but she couldn't speak to explain it to the king. He loved her despite her silence, and asked her to marry him. She nodded, and the ceremony took place. But the old archbishop was becoming suspicious. He said Elisa must be a witch who had beguiled the king. The king refused to believe him.

A few days later, the king led Elisa into a chamber hung with green embroideries. It looked exactly like the cave in the forest. The bundle of nettles and the tunic she had completed were there.

"Will this make you happy, my queen?" he asked.

Elisa smiled. She yearned to confide in her caring husband.

Each night, Elisa stole away to work in her chamber.

The king saw this, and doubt entered his mind. Could she be a witch?

Elisa had begun to knit the final tunic when she ran out of flax. The nettles she needed grew only in the churchyard, so with the moon lighting her way, she slipped out of the palace. The king and the archbishop saw her go, and followed silently behind.

In the churchyard, Elisa thought she saw ghouls wailing and dancing. She shuddered with horror, but her will was strong and she forced herself on.

Watching her, the king concluded she must be dabbling in witchcraft after all. He was broken-hearted. "Let the people judge her," he said sadly.

The next day, the people declared Queen Elisa must be tied to a stake and killed. Crowds jeered as she was carried to the stake in a cart. But Elisa cared more about rescuing her brothers than losing her life. Ten finished tunics lay at her feet. She worked on, even as she travelled, desperate to complete the eleventh.

"Witch!" the mob cried, and tried to pull the tunics away.

Suddenly eleven swans descended, beating their wings to force the crowd back. Elisa's brothers had found her!

As fast as she could, Elisa threw the tunics over the swans, who transformed into eleven princes. The spell had been broken, though the youngest brother still had a wing in place of an arm, as Elisa had not finished the sleeve of his tunic.

"Now I may speak!" she cried. "I am innocent!" Then she fell into her brother's arms.

As the eldest brother told their tale to the crowd, red roses grew up the stake, alongside a single white rose. Full of sorrow and remorse for doubting his wife, the king picked it and held it gently to her face. She opened her eyes and smiled. She had loved him from the beginning; now, at last, she could tell him.

Great flocks of birds appeared, and with the amazed crowd, they followed the king, the queen, and her eleven brothers back to the palace, as church bells rang out in celebration throughout the land.

BEAUTY AND
THE BEAST

There was once a very rich merchant who had three daughters. His youngest daughter was extremely kind; everybody admired her, and called her 'Beauty'. This made her sisters very jealous. They were proud and snobbish, and mocked their younger sister, for she shunned the balls and parties and fine dresses that they loved so much, and instead preferred to spend her time reading in her father's library.

Sadly the merchant lost his fortune. The family became poor, and had to move from their large townhouse with its many rooms and expensive furnishings to a small, simple cottage in the country. The merchant's eldest daughters cried and wailed, but Beauty thought only of her father. 'I am sad to leave behind this library,' she thought to herself, 'but I must help Father in our new life in any way I can.'

Beauty rose at four o'clock each morning to clean the house from top to bottom, feed the chickens and make breakfast. Her two sisters rose late and did nothing but complain about the loss of their fine gowns and suitors.

The family had lived in the cottage for almost a year when the merchant received news of some possible business in a nearby city. When they saw their father ready to set out on his trip, the two eldest daughters begged him to buy them new gowns.

"What do you choose, Beauty?" asked her father. "You must have something from my travels too."

Beauty knew that her sisters' dresses would be costly. "If it's not too much trouble, Father, please bring me a simple rose, for none grow near this cottage."

The merchant went on his journey, but his business deal failed. He left the city as poor as he had entered it. On his way home, it rained and snowed terribly, and he found himself lost in a forest. Night was coming on, and he feared he would freeze to death or else be eaten by the wolves he could hear howling in the darkness. Seeing lights in the distance, he rode his weary horse towards them, and to his surprise found a great illuminated palace.

The merchant tied his horse up in a stable and entered the palace's great hall. Despite the many lit candles, he saw no one, but found a good fire and a table laden with food and wine. He waited and waited, but no servants appeared.

A few hours later, tired and hungry, he could wait no longer. He ate some of the delicious food before finding his way up the sweeping staircase to a magnificent bedchamber, where he slept soundly.

The next morning he woke to find clean clothes and breakfast waiting, yet still no servants. As he went to retrieve his horse, he passed through an arbour of perfect fragrant roses and remembered Beauty's request. Carefully, he picked a handful to take home to her.

Suddenly, there was an almighty roar! A huge beast with twisted horns and great fangs bore down on him. "Ungrateful man!" the Beast growled. "I saved your life by receiving you into my castle, and in return you steal my beloved roses. Well, you shall die for it!"

The merchant fell to his knees. "Please forgive me! I meant no harm – I took them only for my kind, sweet daughter, who asked me to bring her some."

"Daughter?" said the Beast. "Then I will forgive you on one condition: this daughter must come here willingly and stay in the palace. If she refuses, you must return and face your fate."

The merchant had no intention of sacrificing Beauty to the monster, but promised that he himself would return.

"You shall not depart empty-handed," growled the Beast. "There is a great chest in the chamber where you slept. Fill it with whatever you like best."

'Well if I'm going to die,' thought the merchant, 'I shall at least leave my children some wealth.' He filled the great chest with gold and jewels, before hastily leaving the palace.

When the merchant arrived home, he found Beauty waiting patiently for him outside the cottage. Offering his daughter the roses, he fell before her. "Here are your roses, my child, though they will cost me more than you could have ever imagined."

The merchant told of his terrible journey and his promise to the monstrous Beast.

"I will go," said Beauty, who could not bear to think of her father suffering for her sake. "I offer my life for yours."

And though her father tried, she would not be dissuaded.

The next morning Beauty and her father set off. She waved goodbye to her sisters, who pretended to cry at her leaving.

Once at the palace, Beauty and her father entered the great hall. It was set with a splendid feast, though there were no servants to be seen.

An hour later, the Beast appeared. Beauty was terrified, but gathered her courage.

"Have you come here freely?" he growled.

"Y-yes," she replied.

"Then I am grateful," he said. "Merchant, you must leave tomorrow morning and never return. Goodnight, Beauty." With that, he left.

"Oh daughter, I must stay instead!" cried the merchant.

But Beauty insisted, "If you stay, you will be killed. I can face whatever comes for me."

That night Beauty dreamed of a fairy, who said, "Beauty, know that your kindness and bravery shall be rewarded."

When she woke, Beauty told her father about her dream. He was comforted a little, but still wept when he said goodbye.

As soon as he had gone, Beauty wondered whether the Beast would kill her, but she was determined not to be afraid. Instead, she wandered, admiring the palace's fine rooms. She was surprised to find a door that bore her name, and was delighted by the beautiful bedroom inside, complete with a large library. "Would the Beast have given me such a room if he wished to kill me?" she asked herself.

Buoyed with fresh hope, she picked up a book, and words appeared:

> *Welcome, Beauty, banish fear,*
> *You are queen and mistress here;*
> *Speak your wishes, speak your will,*
> *Swift obedience meets them still.*

"Alas," she said, "I desire only to see my poor father."

A great looking glass lit up. To her amazement she saw in it her father arriving home at the cottage. The vision disappeared, but Beauty knew he was safe.

That evening Beauty dined in the great hall. As she ate, the Beast entered. "Beauty, may I join you?"

"As you please," she answered, trembling slightly.

"If you ask me to, I will leave," he said, "for you are mistress here now. But tell me, do you think I am hideous?"

"To some, perhaps," said Beauty, "but you may be good."

"My heart may be good, but I am still a monster." He sighed.

"There are many that deserve that name more than you," Beauty replied. "I prefer you to those who hide an ungrateful heart behind a handsome face."

They talked, and Beauty had almost conquered her dread when he asked, "Beauty, will you be my wife?"

She did not want to make the Beast angry by refusing, but she could not marry someone she did not love, and told him so.

The poor monster turned away. "Then goodnight, Beauty," he said, and walked from the room, looking back at her sadly.

Beauty felt compassion for the poor Beast. She could see the kindness in him, and how lonely he was, and decided she would be his friend.

Beauty spent three months in the palace. Every evening she and the Beast talked, and Beauty found herself looking forward to their time together. He showed her much kindness and would give her fresh roses from the garden. There was only one thing that gave Beauty concern: every night the Beast asked her if she would be his wife. "Beast, I wish I could consent to marry you,"

said Beauty, "but I cannot. I shall always be your most faithful friend – is that not enough?"

"It must be," said the Beast, "though I love you tenderly. If you will not be my wife, will you promise to always stay with me?"

But Beauty had seen another vision of her father in her looking glass, and she knew that he was now very ill. She longed to see him again. "Let me go home and tend to my sick father," she said. "I promise to return in a week, then I will stay here with you for ever."

"Go if you must," said the Beast. "Take this ring, and when you wish to return to me, lay it on your table before you go to bed. But Beauty please, please stay only a week. If you are away any longer, my heart will break and I will die."

When Beauty woke the next morning, she found herself at her father's cottage. He cried with joy to see his dear daughter again! Her sisters were not so delighted. Though their father had used the gold from the Beast to help them find handsome husbands, they were still not satisfied. When they saw that Beauty was as content and lovely as ever, they were sick with envy. She told them of the Beast, and this gave them a wicked idea.

"Sister," said the eldest, "do you think if we keep Beauty here longer than a week, the monster will be so enraged he will kill her?"

"Yes, perhaps he will," agreed the middle sister.

They were so affectionate to poor Beauty that she wept with joy at their seeming kindness. Then they seemed so sad to part with her when the week was at an end, she promised to stay a week longer.

But she could not help thinking of the Beast. She missed him, and found her affection for him had grown. On her tenth night away, she dreamed she was in the palace garden, and that the Beast was dying. She woke crying. The thought of the Beast in agony over her absence made her heart ache. 'I have stayed here too long,' she thought. 'I must return to him. Though he may not be handsome, he is kind and good, and that is what matters most.'

Content that her father's health was much improved, Beauty put her ring on the table, and when she woke the next morning, she was overjoyed to find herself back in the palace. Yet although she searched, the Beast was nowhere to be found.

Beauty feared he was dead, and searched the rooms again in despair. Then she remembered her dream. She ran to the gardens, where she found the poor Beast on the ground.

She knelt down beside him and clasped his great claw. The Beast opened his eyes. "I thought you had forgotten me, and I was in such agony," he rasped. "But seeing you here now, I can die happy."

"No, dear Beast!" cried Beauty. "You must live, for I love you."

Beauty had scarcely finished speaking when the Beast disappeared. In his place lay a handsome prince.

"Long ago a wicked fairy enchanted this castle, and turned me into a Beast," he said. "She told me I must live as a monster until a girl freely gave me her love. Beauty, will you marry me?"

Beauty gave the prince her hand, and they returned to the palace. She was overjoyed to find her father and sisters in the great hall, brought there by the fairy from her dream.

"You value a good heart before beauty," said the fairy, "and your reward will be the true love of this prince." Then she turned to Beauty's sisters. "Your sister's heart is full of warmth and courage;

your hearts are full of malice." And with a swish of her wand they were turned into statues. "You shall stand in the palace and watch your sister's happiness until you realise your folly."

After a magnificent wedding, Beauty and her prince lived a long and happy life together, full of true love and kindness.

HANSEL AND GRETEL

Hansel and Gretel lived in a large forest with their father, who was a woodcutter, and their stepmother. They had always been poor, but things got worse and a time came when there wasn't enough bread to share.

The woodcutter lay awake worrying. "How can we feed my poor children?" he said. "We barely have food for ourselves."

His wife answered, "Listen. Tomorrow we'll take the children deep into the forest and give them each a piece of bread. Then we'll leave them there."

The man protested that he couldn't leave his children to the dangers of the forest, but she insisted he must or they would all starve, and she argued until he agreed.

Lying awake, hungry, the children overheard their stepmother. Gretel began to cry, but Hansel comforted her, "Don't worry, Gretel, I have a plan."

When the others were asleep he crept outside and collected pocketfuls of bright white pebbles.

The next day the stepmother said they would all go into the forest to find wood. She handed Hansel and Gretel a piece of bread each, telling them not to eat it too soon: "This is all there is for lunch." Gretel put the bread in her apron, because Hansel's pockets were full of pebbles.

As they walked through the forest Hansel quietly dropped a bright white pebble at every turn along the path.

They went a long way before their father told them to stop. He made a fire, then the stepmother said, "Children, you stay here and rest. We will go deeper into the forest to chop wood. When we're finished we'll come back for you."

Hansel and Gretel sat by the fire. At midday they ate their bread.

They heard the strokes of an axe and thought their father was nearby. But it wasn't an axe, it was a branch he had tied to a dead tree, so it would sound like chopping when the wind blew it.

As the afternoon drifted on, the children fell asleep waiting, and when they woke it was night. Gretel cried, sure they would never find their home, but Hansel said, "When the moon rises, we'll see the path." Sure enough, the white pebbles he had dropped shone in the moonlight and showed them the way back.

They reached the house at dawn. Their stepmother scolded them for being out all night, but their father was overjoyed to see them.

Soon, though, there was not enough food to go round once more. The stepmother again argued with the woodcutter. "The children must go," she said. "We'll take them even further this time." He felt it would be better to be hungry together, but the stepmother insisted, and he gave in a second time.

The children heard the argument. When his father and stepmother were asleep, Hansel tried to slip out to collect pebbles as he had before, but his stepmother had locked the door. Still he comforted his sister: "Don't cry, Gretel, I will think of something."

The next day as they walked deeper into the forest, Hansel broke his bread into little pieces and dropped the crumbs to mark turns in the path.

They walked all morning, and then their father again made a fire and their stepmother told them to wait: "Rest here, and when we've collected wood we will come back for you." At midday, Gretel shared her piece of bread with Hansel, because his was scattered along the path. As the afternoon drifted on they fell asleep.

When they woke it was dark and no one had come for them. Hansel said, "Wait till the moon rises and the white breadcrumbs will show us the way home."

But they didn't find any breadcrumbs because the birds of the forest had eaten them all.

They walked all night and all the next day and night, but could not find their way home. They kept walking until they were so weak they couldn't go on much further.

They heard a small bird singing beautifully and stopped to listen. Following the music, they found a house in the forest made of gingerbread and sparkling sugar.

"Let's eat some," said Hansel, for they were desperately hungry. He broke a chunk off the roof and Gretel bit the window ledge.

Then a voice from inside called,

Nibble nibble, little mouse,
Who's that nibbling at my house?

The children answered, "It is only the wind."

An old woman hobbled out, saying, "Hello dear children! Don't be afraid, come inside."

She gave them a meal of pancakes, apples and nuts, and Hansel and Gretel thought they were in heaven.

But the old woman was only pretending to be kind. Really, she was a wicked witch who tempted children into her house so she could cook them and eat them up.

The witch bundled Hansel into a shed and locked it. She shouted at Gretel, "Lazy child! You must fetch water and cook. We will fatten up your brother, then I shall eat him!"

Every morning the witch went to the shed to feel how fat Hansel was growing. She told him to hold out his finger, but he stuck out a bone instead. Witches can't see well, and she couldn't tell the difference.

As days passed, she grew tired of waiting and decided to boil him up, fat or not.

"Before the boiling, we'll do some baking," she told Gretel, stoking a blazing fire.

"You lean into the oven to check whether it's hot enough."

The witch was planning to shut Gretel in the oven and roast her. But Gretel guessed her thoughts and said, "I don't know how."

"Stupid child," cried the witch. "It's simple. Look." And she stuck her head in the oven door. Gretel seized her chance. She gave the witch a great push, closed the oven and fastened its bolt. The witch screeched horribly.

Gretel ran from the kitchen and went straight to free her brother. She opened the door of the shed and cried, "Hansel, we're saved! The old witch is dead!"

Hansel hopped out of his prison like a bird from a cage.

How happy they were to be free of the wicked witch! They hugged and kissed each other and danced round and round in celebration.

Now there was nothing to be afraid of, they went back into the witch's house and found boxes overflowing with shining pearls and glittering jewels hidden in the attic. Hansel stuffed his pockets full of them.

Gretel said, "I'll take some too," and filled her little apron with as many as would fit.

"We'd better leave now," said Hansel, "and find a way out of this bewitched forest."

They left the witch's gingerbread house behind and walked for mile after mile, until they came to a wide lake. "How will we get across?" wondered Hansel. "There's no bridge."

"And there's no boat, either," said Gretel, "but over there I see a white duck. I think she'll help us if we ask."

She called to the duck, and sure enough, she took them over the lake, one at a time, on her feathery white back.

When the children were safely across, and had walked further still, the forest looked more familiar, until at last they saw their home in the distance. They began to run, and they flew into the house and threw themselves into their father's arms.

He had been desperately unhappy ever since leaving them in the forest, and in the meantime his wife had died. Seeing his children in front of him now, he was overjoyed.

Gretel opened out her little apron, and the shining pearls and precious stones spilled onto the kitchen table, and Hansel reached into his pockets and pulled out handful after handful of glittering jewels. Their days of hunger and worry were finally over, and together they lived happily ever after.

VASSILISSA

Once, in Russia, there lived a girl of great kindness called Vassilissa.

Her father was a travelling merchant, so Vassilissa and her mother were often alone. When Vassilissa was fourteen, her mother fell ill. "My dearest child," she said, "I am going to die, and then I will not be here to protect you. But take this doll named Koukolka. Look after her well, and she will look after you."

Vassilissa was very sad when her mother died, but she kept her doll close.

Vassilissa's father didn't want her to be by herself when he travelled, so he married a widow who had two daughters of her own. He did not understand that Vassilissa's stepmother and stepsisters were cruel. They were jealous of Vassilissa and hated her kindness. As soon as her father went away, they dressed her in rags and made her work hard all day.

But Vassilissa had a friend: her doll, Koukolka. Every evening, secretly, she cared for Koukolka and brought her small gifts. She would tell Koukolka her troubles, and the doll always gave her wise advice and comfort. Every day, once the others went out, Koukolka helped Vassilissa. Though she was small, Koukolka could do mountains of work in the blink of an eye. She would tell Vassilissa to rest for an hour; meanwhile water was carried, the oven was warmed, the vegetable patch was weeded, the soup was simmered and all the beds were made.

Years passed. The stepsisters aimed to marry, but no one wanted them, and they blamed Vassilissa.

"Everyone thinks Vassilissa is so fair and kind," they complained. "How are we to find suitors when no one notices us?"

They decided to get rid of her.

Behind Vassilissa's house was a dark forest. Everyone knew that the witch Baba Yaga lived in a cottage in the forest, and that she ate human flesh. Vassilissa's stepmother sent her to find firewood again and again. She hoped the girl would stumble upon the witch and never return, but Vassilissa kept Koukolka hidden in her pocket, and the doll always showed her a safe path home.

One evening, the stepdaughters were knitting and sewing while Vassilissa spun yarn. The stepmother quietly put out the fire and every candle except the one beside the girls. Then she opened a window so a gust of wind blew that one out too.

"It is late, but your work is not finished," she said. "There's no fire in the house, but Baba Yaga will still be awake. One of you must go and ask her for a flame to relight the candle."

"I don't need to light the candle," said her eldest daughter. "My knitting needles glimmer in the dark."

"Nor do I," said her sister. "My sewing needle shines."

"Vassilissa, you must go," said all three.

Vassilissa ran to her doll Koukolka. "They are sending me to Baba Yaga!" she cried. "The witch will eat me."

"Be brave, Vassilissa," said her doll. "Carry me with you, but make sure I am hidden. I will keep you safe."

It was a long walk through the dark, windy forest. At last Vassilissa reached Baba Yaga's cottage. Its fence was made from human bones topped with glowing skulls. Vassilissa felt so frightened she couldn't move.

Baba Yaga opened the door, sniffing the air. "Do I smell a human? Who's there?"

"It's only me – Vassilissa," replied the trembling girl. "My stepmother sent me to fetch a flame."

"Ah yes, I know you, Vassilissa. I will give you some fire," cackled the witch, her giant teeth shining like knives. "But first you must stay and work for me for three days. If you fail, I will eat you." She pulled the girl inside the cottage.

The first day, the witch gave Vassilissa enough work for three servants: millet to sift, corn to grind, the yard to sweep, bones to polish, and a great dinner to cook. Baba Yaga gave instructions, then went out in her giant mortar, paddling through the air with the pestle and her broom.

Vassilissa collapsed in despair, but Koukolka told her to cook the dinner then rest. The doll quickly sifted, ground, swept and polished. All was complete when Baba Yaga returned hungry.

"Such a wonderful tasty pie!" declared the witch, before she fell asleep.

The second day, Baba Yaga gave Vassilissa enough work for five servants.

As soon as she flew off, Koukolka quickly stitched and stuffed a goose-feather quilt, beat the rugs and polished the windows while Vassilissa baked.

All was complete when the witch returned. "Delicious," she grunted, eating the last crumbs of a fine cheesecake. And she went to sleep rolled up in the new quilt.

On the third day the witch gave Vassilissa enough work for ten servants. As well as ordering Vassilissa to scrub the floors, mend her stockings and sweep the stairs, Baba Yaga showed her a huge sack of wheat mixed with dirt. "You must pick out every grain," she said, "then cook me a feast of pigs and apples!"

Once the witch had flown off in her mortar and pestle, Vassilissa brought small gifts to Koukolka, and cried.

"Dry your tears," said Koukolka. "A bit of work will solve it all. You cook, then rest. I will sort the grain." And she did, as well as scrubbing, mending and sweeping.

"I do not understand it," growled Baba Yaga when she returned. "The more work I give you, the more you do. But I will keep my word."

When she had gobbled her rich feast of stuffed pig and baked apples, she called the girl. "I must let you go, young Vassilissa, but answer me one question first: how do you finish all the work I give you?"

Vassilissa kept Koukolka hidden in her pocket. "My mother's blessing helps me," she replied.

"Ah, I see." The witch nodded. "Well, be off with you. The blessed are disgusting to me. Take this: its eyes will light your candle." The witch grabbed a stick topped with a glowing skull from her fence, and handed it to Vassilissa.

Vassilissa gathered her courage and walked through the forest all night carrying the skull lantern.

When she arrived home, no lights shone from the windows. Her stepmother and stepsisters had been without any fire since she'd left. The eldest stepsister had brought hot embers from a neighbour, but they went cold as soon as they were inside the house.

When Vassilissa first stepped indoors with the fire in the skull, her stepmother was pleased. "What? Vassilissa! Ah! You have brought a light…" But the glowing eyes from the witch's fencepost stared unblinking at the stepmother and stepdaughters, growing hotter and hotter, until the whole house began to burn!

Vassilissa was the only one who stepped out alive. She buried the skull and walked to the nearest town.

There she found an old woman who lived alone, who agreed to take her in until her father returned from his travels.

Once she was settled, Vassilissa asked the old woman to buy some flax so she could spin it and make a fine cloth. The woman bought the best flax at the market. Vassilissa took great pleasure in spinning it into fine thread.

Koukolka told her to find an old weaver's comb, a weaving shuttle and some horsehair. From them, Koukolka built the perfect loom.

Vassilissa worked spinning and weaving all winter, until she had armfuls of beautiful linen cloth, which she made into a dozen soft white shirts.

"Take these and sell them as thanks for giving me a safe home," she said to the old woman.

"The Tsar alone is worthy of shirts this fine," the woman objected. "I will present them to him as a gift."

She took Vassilissa's shirts to the palace, where the young Tsar was so delighted with them, he asked to thank the seamstress in person.

As soon as he and Vassilissa laid eyes on one another, they knew they would never want to be apart. They were married with great celebration, and when Vassilissa's father came home he was stunned to find her living in the palace! Now that she was well provided for, he no longer needed to travel, and he lived near his daughter all the rest of his days. The old woman stayed close by her too.

Vassilissa kept Koukolka closest of all. Before she died, she gave the doll to her own daughter, just in case.

THE AUTHORS

VASSILISSA

Alexander Nikolayevich Afanasyev (1826–1871) was a Russian scholar and historian, most famous for recording and publishing over 600 traditional folk and fairy tales. One of the largest collections of folklore in the world, this work earned him a reputation as the 'Russian Brother Grimm'. His *Russian Fairy Tales* compilation was banned in Russia until 1914.

THE WILD SWANS

Hans Christian Andersen (1805–1875) was a Danish author, best known for writing fairy tales that could be enjoyed by children. His stories, including 'The Little Mermaid', 'The Princess and the Pea' and 'The Emperor's New Clothes', are some of the best-loved tales in the world. His works have been translated into more than 125 languages and inspired countless plays, ballets, books and films.

THE SPIRIT IN THE BOTTLE, THE THREE GOLDEN HAIRS & HANSEL AND GRETEL

Jacob (1785–1863) and **Wilhelm Grimm** (1786–1859), together known as the Brothers Grimm, were German professors who created the most famous collection of folk and fairy tales in the world. Jacob and Wilhelm recorded and adapted folk tales that were once exclusively part of an oral tradition. Their best-known stories, including 'Snow White', 'Sleeping Beauty' and 'Rapunzel', are still iconic more than two hundred years after they were first published.

BEAUTY AND THE BEAST

Jeanne-Marie Leprince de Beaumont (1711–1780) was a prolific French author most famous for her popular adaptation of 'Beauty and the Beast' from the original by Gabrielle-Suzanne Barbot de Villeneuve. Jeanne-Marie was married to an infamous French spy and her life was fictionalised in the novel *Crossings*.

THE SELFISH GIANT

Oscar Wilde (1854–1900) was a celebrated Irish novelist, poet and playwright, and one of the most controversial writers of his time. He wrote the fairy tale collection *The Happy Prince and Other Tales* for his sons.

THE ILLUSTRATOR

Scott Plumbe was born on the west coast of Canada. He is an award-winning illustrator, designer and fine artist whose work appears in books, games and magazines including *National Geographic Kids*. He lives in Vancouver with his young family.

STUNNING FOLK AND FAIRY TALE COLLECTIONS

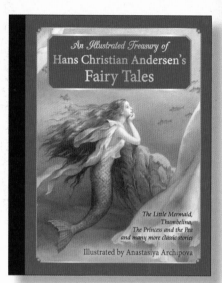

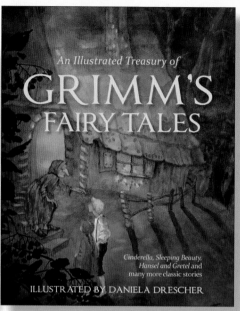

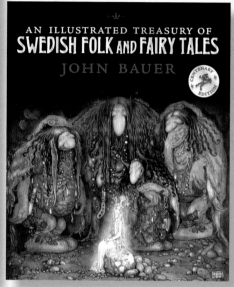

'A wonderfully entertaining collection... Unreservedly recommended.'

MIDWEST BOOK REVIEW

on *An Illustrated Treasury of Swedish Folk and Fairy Tales*

'Timeless stories presented in a beautifully illustrated book to keep forever.'

CREATIVE STEPS

on *An Illustrated Treasury of Hans Christian Andersen's Fairy Tales*

'A traditional and satisfying compilation.'

THE WALL STREET JOURNAL

on *An Illustrated Treasury of Grimm's Fairy Tales*

florisbooks.co.uk

ENCHANTING STORIES FROM SCOTLAND

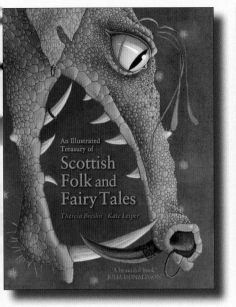
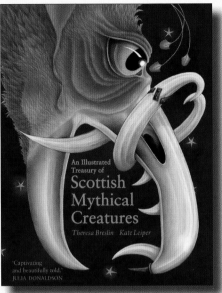

PRAISE FOR THE SERIES

'A sublime collection of folk stories... Theresa Breslin's pristine, sparkline retellings are accompanied by enchanting illustrations from Kate Leiper.'

THE GUARDIAN

'Lively yarn-spinning, delightful illustrations, and handsome bookmaking again make a winning combination.'

KIRKUS REVIEWS

'A harmonious braiding of pitch-perfect storytelling with illustrations of breathtaking elegance and integrity. Every home should have at least one copy.'

DEBI GLIORI

'Breslin brings an array of creatures to life with her assured and captivating storytelling, which places a child at the heart of each tale.'

JULIA DONALDSON

florisbooks.co.uk